The Alligator in the Library

Written by Suzanne Hodson

Illustrated by Jaimee Christensen

Jordan and his mother were making their first trip to the library in their new town.

"See, Jordan?" said Mother. "Here is the checkout desk, where we get our library card and check out our books." Mother stopped at the desk to get a card. Jordan looked around.

"Mama, alligator!" whispered Jordan, pointing to the big elevator.

"You mean elevator," said Mother. "Come on, let's go find some fun picture books to read."

Jordan and Mother looked at the picture books and found five to take home. "Now I need to go downstairs to get a book," said Mother.

Mother took Jordan's hand and walked toward the stairs. Jordan looked at the elevator.

"Alligator!"

"Elevator," Mother corrected. "But we will take the stairs."

After mother found two books, she said,
"Let's go upstairs and look at the videos."
Jordan stared at the elevator.

"I know you want to ride in the elevator," said Mother, "but I like to get my exercise."

"Alligator!" said Jordan, pointing.

"Elevator!" Mother insisted.

While mother picked a video and some tapes, Jordan watched a big TV.

When Mother came to get Jordan, he grabbed her hand and pulled her toward the elevator.

"Alligator! Alligator!" he cried.

"Oh, Jordan, I've told you it's an EL-E-VA-TOR! Say 'EL-E-VA-TOR.'"

"Look! Alligator!" squealed Jordan. Mother shook her head and tugged Jordan down the stairs.

At the checkout desk, Mother checked out the video, books, and tapes. Jordan helped carry his books.

"Next week maybe we can come to storytime," said Mother. "And maybe I will let you ride the el-e-va-tor."

Jordan looked back.

"Bye-bye, Alligator!" he said.

electronic education

SF
AW

READ·ALONG

8

9 780201 330076

90000

ISBN   0-201-33007-5

Jade's Note

Written by **Cynthia Belnap**

Illustrated by **Hala Day**

Developed by Waterford Institute, Inc., Sandy, Utah.
Waterford Institute is a nonprofit research center whose mission is to enable every child to receive the finest education possible by providing high-quality educational models, programs, and software.

Published and distributed by Electronic Education, Sunnyvale, California.
Electronic Education is dedicated to enriching the learning experience for all students with innovative and effective programs that will prepare them for success in the 21st century.

Printed in the United States of America.

ISBN 0-201-47837-4

4 5 6 7 8 9 10 11 12 13 14 15 16 17 18 19 20-CAS-10 09 08 07 06 05 04 03 02